THE CHEESE CHASE

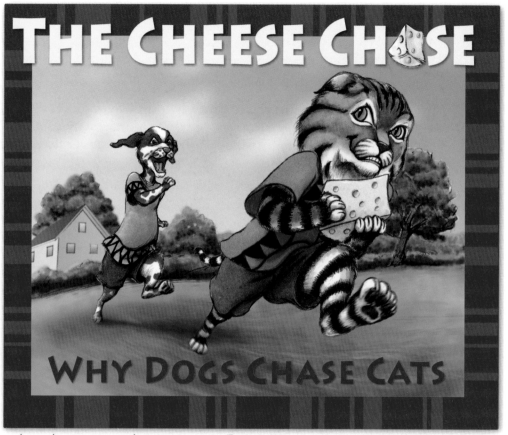

WHY DOGS CHASE CATS

AN AFRICAN-AMERICAN FOLK TALE RETOLD BY TONI SIMMONS

ILLUSTRATED BY BRIAN WOLF

Beaver's Pond Press, Inc.
Edina, Minnesota

ISBN 1-59298-059-7

Library of Congress Catalog Number: 2004xxxxxx

Book design and typesetting: Mori Studio
Cover design: Mori Studio
Illustrated by Brian Wolf

Printed in the United States of America

First Printing: September 2003

06 05 04 03   6 5 4 3 2 1

Beaver's Pond Press, Inc.   7104 Ohms Lane, Suite 216
Edina, MN 55439
(952) 829-8818
www.BeaversPondPress.com

to order, visit *www.BookHouseFulfillment.com* or call
1-800-901-3480. Reseller discounts available.

This book
is dedicated to
my loving husband, Frank
for his continued encouragement
and support of my work.

My sincere thanks to him
for making this book possible.

Author's Note

As a storyteller, I have had much fun telling this story and have found it to be quite enjoyable to young children. As a former children's librarian, I thought it would be great as a read-aloud. So to bring to life this delightful tale of sharing and friendship, and to offer it to the widest audience possible, I have combined my oral telling with Brian Wolf's fanciful artwork to render this picture book.

The story of "Why Dogs Chase Cats" or "Why the Dog Hates the Cat" comes from African-American folklore, having appeared in print form, much earlier, in Zora Neale Hurston's *Mules and Men.* As is true of most folktales, there are other variants of the tale, as well, such as the one found in Julius Lester's collection of folktales, *Knee-High Man and Other Tales.*

The cheese chant that I have included is designed to encourage participation from the readers and listeners.

It is my hope that you will find as much pleasure reading and sharing Cat and Dog's story as I have with hundreds of others over the years.

Toni Simmons

DOG AND CAT USED TO BE GOOD FRIENDS.

THEY DID EVERYTHING TOGETHER.

THEY WERE BEST BUDDIES.

THEY PLAYED BASKETBALL TOGETHER.

THEY WERE ON THE SAME SOCCER TEAM.

THEY WALKED HOME
FROM SCHOOL TOGETHER.

They ate their favorite snack together.

Cheese, cheese, cheese!

One day, Dog reached in his pocket.

He pulled out some money.

"Cat!" he said. "I've got fifty cents.

Do you have
   any money?"

Cat reached in his pocket.

He pulled out some money.

"Dog!" he said. "I've got fifty cents, too."

Dog said, "Let's put our money together. Let's go to the store and buy a big fat piece of Cheese, cheese, cheese!" That's just what they did.

THE STORE WAS FULL OF ALL KINDS OF CHEESE, COLBY, SWISS, CHEDDAR AND COTTAGE. DOG AND CAT COULDN'T DECIDE WHICH ONE TO BUY. THEY ONLY HAD ONE DOLLAR.

THEY FINALLY BOUGHT A NICE MEDIUM CHUNK OF SWISS CHEESE.

DOG SAID, "LET'S WAIT AND EAT THE CHEESE WHEN WE GET HOME. WE'LL TAKE TURNS CARRYING IT. I'LL GO FIRST."

Dog put the cheese in his paw.

He walked down the road with his friend Cat.

Dog decided to sing. It would make the time go faster.

"Cheese, cheese!

I'm carrying our cheese.

Cheese, Cheese!

I'm carrying our cheese."

THEN DOG STOPPED. HE GAVE THE CHEESE TO CAT AND SAID,
"NOW IT'S YOUR TURN."
"YOU CAN CARRY IT."

So Cat took the cheese and put it in his paw.

He walked right beside his friend Dog.

He sang,
"Cheese, Cheese!
I'm carrying my cheese.
Cheese, Cheese!
I'm carrying my cheese.

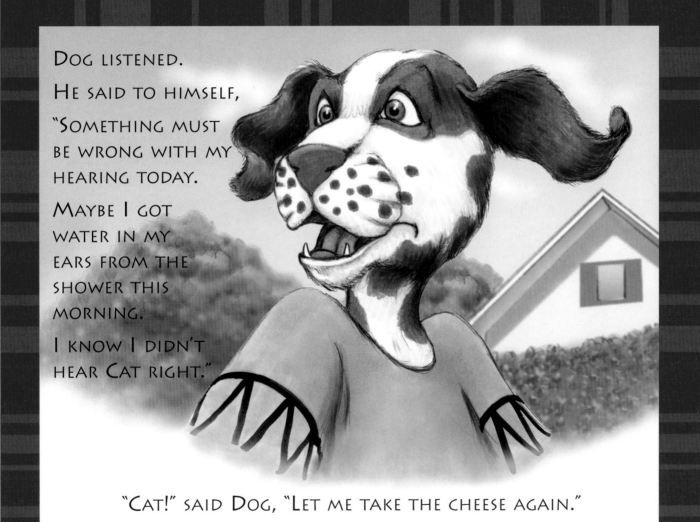

DOG LISTENED.
HE SAID TO HIMSELF,
"SOMETHING MUST
BE WRONG WITH MY
HEARING TODAY.

MAYBE I GOT
WATER IN MY
EARS FROM THE
SHOWER THIS
MORNING.

I KNOW I DIDN'T
HEAR CAT RIGHT."

"CAT!" SAID DOG, "LET ME TAKE THE CHEESE AGAIN."

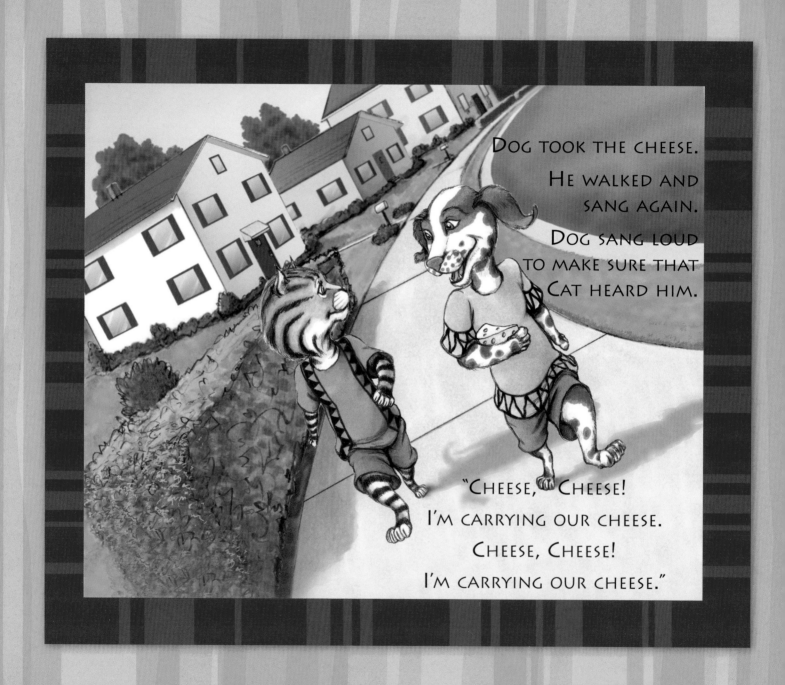

Then Dog said, "Now Cat, we are almost home.
You take it the rest of the way."
Cat said, "Okay."
So, he took the cheese and the two friends walked together.

Dog stopped.

"Cat!" he said. "Why are you singing YOUR cheese?"

Did you forget? We put our money together.
Did you forget? We are going to share!"

SUDDENLY, CAT TOOK OFF RUNNING DOWN THE STREET WITH THE CHEESE.

HE RAN AND HE RAN.

DOG RAN AFTER HIM SHOUTING,

"WHERE ARE YOU GOING WITH OUR CHEESE?"

CAT CAME TO A TREE.

HE CLIMBED IT.

DOG JUMPED
AND BARKED.

HE COULD NOT
CLIMB THE TREE.

HE LOOKED
UP AT CAT.

CAT LOOKED DOWN ON DOG.

THEN ATE THE CHEESE RIGHT IN FRONT OF DOG!

DOG SAID, "HOW COULD YOU?

CAT LICKED HIS PAWS.
"I WAS HUNGRIER THAN YOU.
IT WAS JUST A SMALL PIECE
OF CHEESE."

Dog said, "No, it wasn't.
It was a medium piece of cheese.
Enough for two.
We were friends.
We were going to share."

Cat said teasingly, "Na, na, na, na! I won and you lost!"

"No, Cat!" Dog said.

"I only lost a piece of cheese.
You lost a friend."

EVER SINCE THEN,
DOG HAS NEVER FORGIVEN CAT.
THAT'S WHY DOGS CHASE CATS.

About The Author

After years of working as a children's librarian and drama teacher, Toni Simmons combined her talents and began traveling the nation sharing stories. Her listeners become a part of her multicultural oral traditions with carefully orchestrated rhythms, chants and movements. Toni has performed throughout the United States in South Africa and Germany. She is a Touring Artist for the Texas Commission on the Arts and the Louisiana Division of the Arts and is listed on the Arts Midwest Heartland Fund. Her video "Stories Alive! African and African-American Folktales" won a Parents' Choice and Parent Council Award. It received recommended reviews by Booklist and School Library Journal.

Toni received a Bachelor of Arts degree from Fisk University and a Master of Library Science from Atlanta University. She is the mother of two sons, Brian and Mark. Toni and her husband Frank reside in Minneapolis and Dallas.

About The Illustrator

Brian Wolf was born and raised in Madison, Wisconsin and graduated from the University of Wisconsin-Madison with a BA in Marketing and a minor in Art. He currently lives in Minneapolis, Minnesota and has been a self-employed commercial illustrator for fifteen years.

"I have always had a deep appreciation for the art of children's books—the imaginative storytelling and vast depth of imagery. It's a world unto itself. I have long wanted to venture into the field and, in recent years, have studied writing in addition to my illustration interests. I was happy to have *The Cheese Chase* be my first step into the world of children's book illustration."

for more stories, visit

www.tonisimmons.com